Melvin the Mouth

Katherine Blanc

Illustrated by
Jeffrey Ebbeler

Charlesbridge

For Noel Blanc, who made his dad, Mel Blanc, very proud—K. B.

For my dad, who loved Yosemite Sam—J. E.

Published by Charlesbridge
85 Main Street
Watertown, MA 02472
(617) 926-0329
www.charlesbridge.com

Library of Congress Cataloging-in-Publication Data
Names: Blanc, Katherine, author. | Ebbeler, Jeffrey, illustrator.
Title: Melvin the Mouth / Katherine Blanc ; illustrated by Jeffrey Ebbeler.
Description: Watertown, MA : Charlesbridge, [2017] | A story based on the childhood of Mel Blanc, father-in-law of
   the author, and voice of characters like Woody Woodpecker and many others. | Summary: Melvin the Mouth
   cannot resist making a variety of strange noises as he imagines himself as a dragon, a shark, or perhaps a train—but
   his talent gets him into trouble at school.
Identifiers: LCCN 2016009221 (print) | LCCN 2016012262 (ebook) | ISBN 9781580897143 (reinforced for library use) |
   ISBN 9781607348740 (ebook) | ISBN 9781607348757 (ebook pdf)
Subjects: LCSH: Blanc, Mel—Childhood and youth—Juvenile fiction. | Imagination—Juvenile fiction. | Sounds—
   Juvenile fiction. | Schools—Juvenile fiction. | CYAC: Blanc, Mel—Childhood and youth—Fiction. |
   Imagination—Fiction. | Sounds—Fiction. | Schools—Fiction.
Classification: LCC PZ7.1.B6 Me 2017 (print) | LCC PZ7.1.B6 (ebook) | DDC [E]—dc23
LC record available at https://lccn.loc.gov/2016009221

Printed in China
(hc) 10 9 8 7 6 5 4 3 2 1

Illustrations done on Fabriano Artistico hot-press watercolor paper,
   then combined with ink drawings in Photoshop
Display type hand-lettered by Jeffrey Ebbeler
Text type set in Dante MT by The Monotype Corporation
Color separations by Colourscan Print Co Pte Ltd, Singapore
Printed by 1010 Printing International Limited in
   Huizhou, Guangdong, China
Production supervision by Brian G. Walker
Designed by Martha MacLeod Sikkema

ha

ha

Ha Hay ho!

I'm flying over the cat,
laughing like a loony bird. I'm Melvin the
Mouth, maker of sounds.

"Melvin, let's go," Mom calls.
I'm dressed, except for my shoes. I'm a dragon—and dragons have bare feet.

"Melvin, my dear dragon," Mom says, "*please* put on your shoes."

At school I run into the main hallway. It's a tunnel with tile walls—perfect for making BIG sounds.

I can't help myself. Whenever I'm in that hallway, I open my mouth and . . .

. . . I'm a tiger roaming in a deep cave, looking for people to eat. I stomp my feet, flash my teeth, and roar.

No one can escape—unless I let them.

In the boys' room I'm a giant shark swimming through a coral reef. I stalk my prey and snap my jaws.

"Be quiet, quiet, QUIET!" my teacher yells.

If only I were a real shark.

After lunch I'm a train zooming through the tunnel. Watch out, everybody!

I slam right into the school principal.

"Melvin!" she shouts. "Close that mouth! No recess for you. You're on trash duty!"

But I can't let her spoil my fun.

On the playground I'm a truck scooping up tons of junk. I'm too slow, so I change into a race car. I speed through the dust, screeching around corners.

The playground lady holds up her hand. I hit the brakes. She gives me a speeding ticket.

"Ask your parents to sign this paper and send it back tomorrow," she says.

But I'm still the fastest mouth in the world.

The school bus rumbles and bounces like a rocket in space, hurtling faster and faster toward Earth. It's a rough ride, so I warn the crew in my robot voice:

Pre·pare for land·ing.

Five.

Four.

Three.

Two.

One!

"Melvin the Mouth, that is enough out of you," says the bus driver.

"Melvin," Mom says when I give her my speeding ticket, "that mouth of yours causes problems. Bring in the groceries." I am Melvin the Mouth, and I can be *very* helpful. I'm a dump truck—stronger than my big brother. I drive backward honking my horn. I almost hit the cat.

"Thank you, Melvin," says Mom. "Now sweep the floor."

I'm a tornado, swirling and whirling. Watch out, everybody. Here I come!

"Enough sweeping," Mom says. "Now you can rake the yard."

Grrrrrrrrr!

A rabbit is digging in Mom's garden.
But I'm a big scary dog.
And I'll run that rabbit out of town.

Grrrrrrrr!

Oops. Sorry, plants.
Mom calls me in for dinner.
She doesn't sound happy.

I'm a huge hungry hippopotamus. My mouth opens wide.

"Well done, Melvin the Mouth," Dad says. "You were a big help around the house. But no more problems at school, okay?"

"I'll try, Dad. And sorry about the garden, Mom," I say.

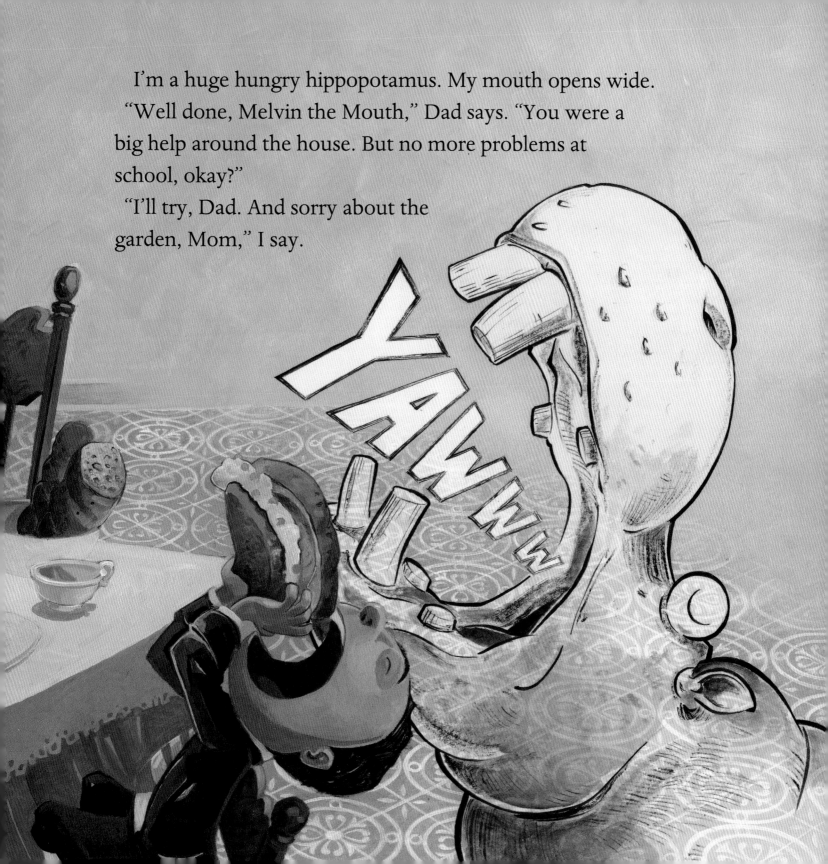

After dinner a storm churns the waters. A ship is sinking.
I'm a strong tugboat, towing it to safety.
"Time to get out of the tub," Mom says.
I saved the ship!

In my snug pajamas I'm a dragon once again.
I burrow under my covers, guarding the
entrance to my den.
I am running out of steam. I'm a *sleepy* dragon.

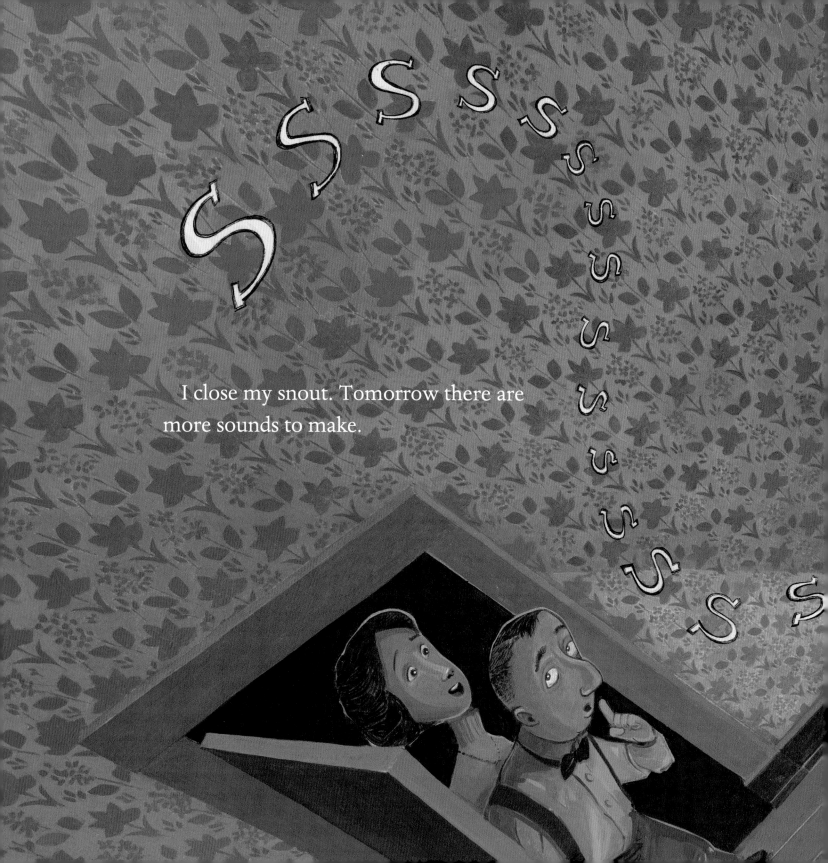

I close my snout. Tomorrow there are more sounds to make.

AUTHOR'S NOTE

For many years I've wanted to share the story of how my father-in-law, Melvin "Mel" Blanc (1908–1989), discovered his "magic mouth" as a child in Portland, Oregon.

As Melvin grew up, he created thousands of sounds and voices, which made his friends and family laugh (and sometimes annoyed them). Melvin got into trouble at school because of his constant sound effects. But his parents were always supportive, and he knew that one day he would make a living as a voice actor. Nobody could have realized how famous he would become. Although Mel died in 1989, his voices are still heard every day by millions of people around the world.

Known as the "Man of 1,000 Voices," Mel Blanc actually created more than 1,500 different characters for Hollywood movies, television, and radio. But Mel is most famous for his Looney Tunes® and Hanna-Barbera cartoon voices: Bugs Bunny, Daffy Duck, Porky Pig, Sylvester and Tweety, the Tasmanian Devil, Marvin the Martian, Barney Rubble, and so many more.

And remember Melvin's crazy laugh—**Ha-ha-ha-HAY-ho!**—at the beginning of this book? Many years later that same laugh became the famous sound of Woody Woodpecker.